GUMMY JOKE 英文軟糖笑話 2

BÜT
i LIKE

點子出版
IDEA PUBLICATION

The Benefits of JOKES

Boost Confidence!
提升自信

Be Confidence! Making people laugh boosts self-esteem and brings a sense of accomplishment.
讓人發笑可以提高自信心，並帶來成就感！

Icebreaker!
破冰者

Starting conversations! Always a great way to initiate conversation in social situations.
在社交場合中，總是開啟對話的最佳「武器」！

Cultural Exchange!
文化交流

Sharing jokes from different cultures broadens minds and brings us closer with a laugh!
分享來自不同文化的笑話開闊思維，讓我們在笑聲中更親近！

Spark Curiosity!
童年回憶

Jokes spark curiosity by surprising you, making you want to uncover the real meaning!

笑話帶來驚奇，讓你充滿好奇，迫不及待想找出背後的真相！

Reduces Stress!
減輕壓力

Jokes reduce stress by triggering laughter, releasing endorphins, and helping you relax.

笑話像魔法一樣，釋放快樂安多酚，壓力全都飛走！

Quick Thinking!
轉數快

Think fast! Jokes boost quick thinking, especially when you're on the spot and need to think fast!

笑話讓你腦袋轉得超快，尤其是在急中生智的時候！

Contents

GUMMY Joke 英文軟糖笑話 2

Contents

GUMMY JOKE 英文軟糖笑話 2

Contents

GUMMY Joke 英文軟糖笑話 2

Contents

GUMMY Joke 英文軟糖笑話 2

Contents

GUMMY
Joke 英文軟糖笑話 2

FLIP AND LAUGH
but i like
001 - 020

001 - 020

Egg On Vacation
Vampire's Favourite
Talkative Flower
Charity
Rain's Accessory
Harvest Favorite
No-Entry
Classroom King
Dream Car
Counting Creatures
Scented Insect
Pasta Peace
Barking Band
Too Hot
Writer's Choice
Fish Show
No-Dog Zone
Hungry Mermaid
Nut Decor
Injured Pizza

001
Egg On Vacation

Where's an egg's favorite vacation spot?

- Select Your Answer! -

A Japan

B New York City

C Hawaii

001 ANSWER
B
New
York City
(New Yolk City)

002
Vampire's Favorite

What is a vampire's least favourite day of the week?

- Select Your Answer! -

A	B	C
Tuesday	Friday	Sunday

002 ANSWER
C
Sunday
(Sun-day)

003
Talkative Flower

Which flower talks the most?

- Select Your Answer! -

A Tulip

B Rose

C Lily

003 ANSWER
A
Tulip
(Two-lip)

004
Charity

Why don't lobsters donate to charity?

- Select Your Answer! -

A
They are rich.

B
They are weak.

C
They are shellfish.

004 ANSWER
C
They are shellfish.
(Selfish)

005
Rain's Accessory

What is rain's favorite accessory?

- Select Your Answer! -

A Hat

B Bow

C Tie

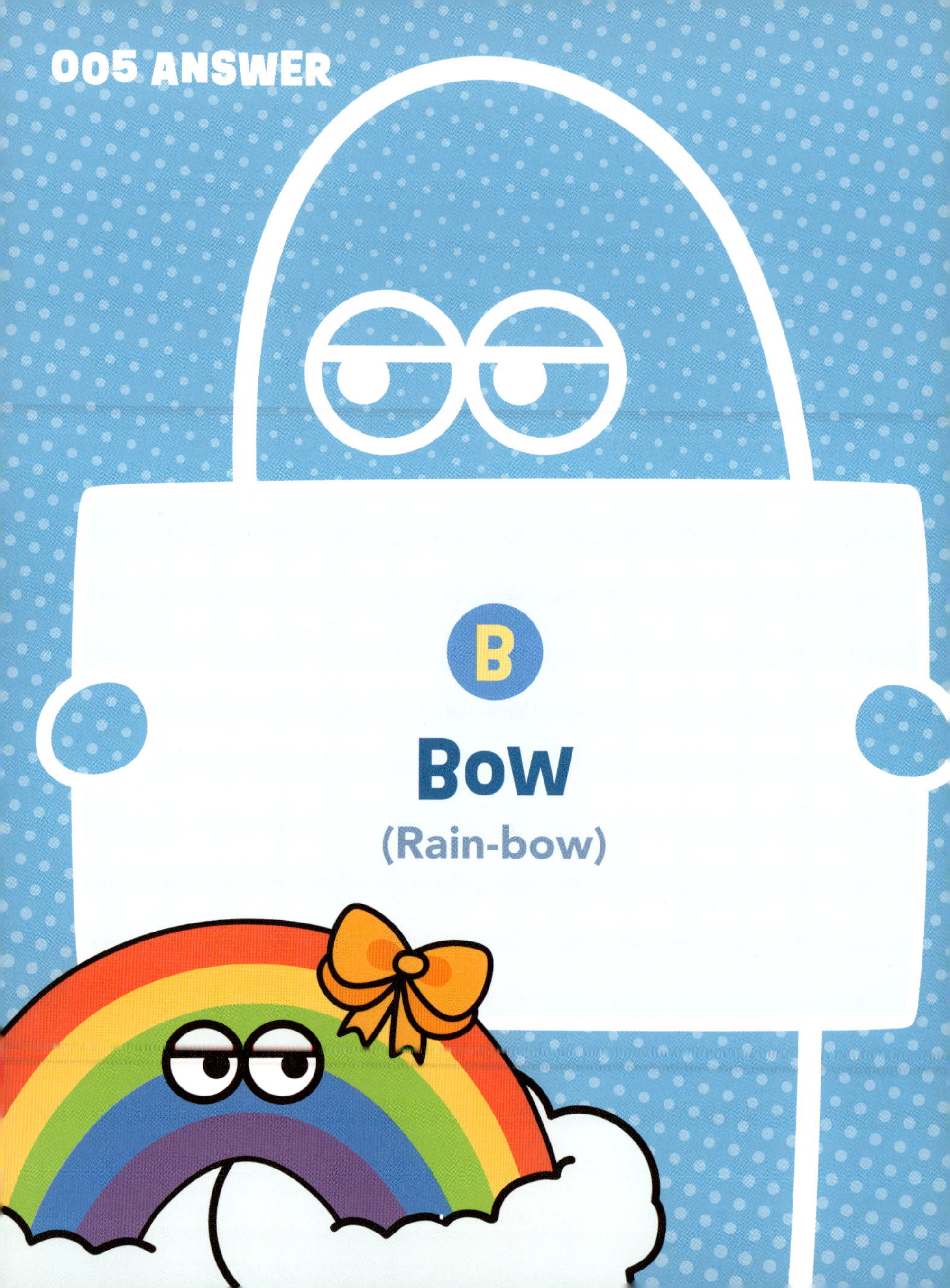
005 ANSWER
B
Bow
(Rain-bow)

006
Harvest Favorite

What is a scarecrow's favorite fruit?

- Select Your Answer! -

A	B	C
Apple	Strawberry	Peach

006 ANSWER
B
Strawberry
(Straw-berry)

007
No-Entry

What room are ghosts not allowed to enter?

- Select Your Answer! -

A Bathroom

B Bedroom

C Living Room

007 ANSWER
C
Living
Room

008
Classroom King

Which stationary is the King of the classroom?

- Select Your Answer! -

Ruler

Eraser

C
Highlighter

008 ANSWER
A
Ruler

009
Dream Car

What kind of car does a sheep like to drive?

- Select Your Answer! -

Tesla

Mini cooper

Lamborghini

009 ANSWER
C
Lamb-orghini
LAMB-ORGHINI

010

Counting Creatures

What sea creature can add up?

- Select Your Answer! -

A Shark

B Octopus

C Dolphins

010 ANSWER
B
Octo-plus

011

Scented Insect

What's the best smelling insect?

- Select Your Answer! -

A Butterfly

B Ant

C Bee

011 ANSWER

012
Pasta Peace

What's the most relaxing type of pasta?

- Select Your Answer! -

Spaghetti

Lasagna

Macaroni

012 ANSWER
A
SPA-ghetti

013
Barking Band

What's a dog's favorite instrument?

- Select Your Answer! -

A	B	C
Saxophone	Violin	Trombone

013 ANSWER
C
Trom-BONE

014

Too Hot

What is the spiciest country to visit?

- Select Your Answer! -

A Australia

B Chile

C Spain

014 ANSWER
B
Chile
(Chili)

015

Writer's Choice

Which stationery confused Shakespeare the most?

- Select Your Answer! -

Pencil

Marker

Chalk

015 ANSWER
A
Pencil
confused him.
2B or not 2B?
(To be or not to be)
HB
2B

016
Fish Show

What's the best way to watch a fishing show?

- Select Your Answer! -

A Podcast

B Cinemas

C Live Stream

016 ANSWER
LIVE
C
Live Stream

017
No-Dog Zone

Where's a place you should never take a dog?

- Select Your Answer! -

A
Flea Market

B
Library

C
Bowling Alley

017 ANSWER

018
Hungry Mermaid

What's a mermaid's favorite meal?

- Select Your Answer! -

A	B	C
Pizza	Tiramisu	Sandwich

018 ANSWER
C
Sand-wich

019
Nut Decor

What kind of nuts hangs on the wall?

- Select Your Answer! -

A Walnut

B Almonds

C Pistachio

019 ANSWER

A

Walnut!

(Wall-nut!)

020
Injured Pizza

How do you fix a broken pizza?

- Select Your Answer! -

A Pineapple

B Tomato Paste

C Cheese

020 ANSWER
B
Tomato
Paste

MEMO

BUT I LIKE

GUMMY
Joke 英文軟糖笑話 2

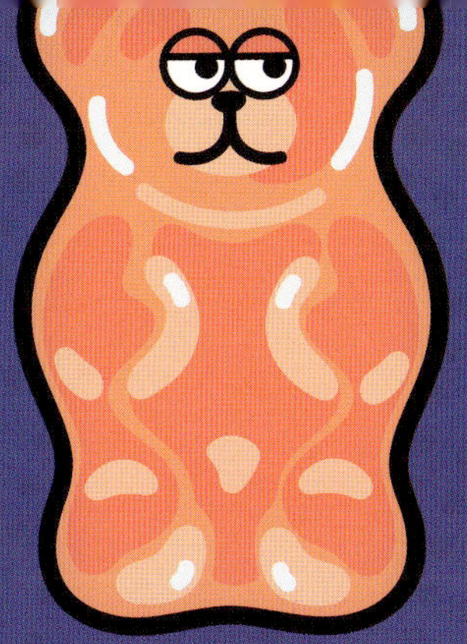

JOKES AND GIGGLES

021. Moon Meal

What do you think of that new diner on the moon?

Food was good, but there wasn't much atmosphere.

LIKE REPLY

022. Word Puzzle

What begins with P, ends with E, and has 1,000 letters?

Post office.

LIKE REPLY

Vocabulary Corner 實用詞彙

Meal 餐	Atmosphere 氣氛	Begin 開始

023. Bad Breath

How does a scientist freshen his breath?

With experi-mints.

LIKE REPLY

024. Dirt Brew

Why did the coffee taste like dirt?

Because it was ground just a few minutes ago.

LIKE REPLY

Scientist 科學家	Freshen 變清新	Brew 冲咖啡	Dirt 塵土

025. Falling Figures

When do accountants fall over?

When they lose their balance.

LIKE REPLY

026. Rich Breath

What's the best air to breathe if you want to be rich?

Millionaire.

LIKE REPLY

Vocabulary Corner
實用詞彙

Accountant
會計師

Balance
平衡

Rich
富有

027. Salesman Cat

Why are cats the best salesman?

They are very purr-suasive.

LIKE REPLY

028. Hot drink

How do you ask a dinosaur for a hot drink?

Tea, Rex? (T-Rex)

LIKE REPLY

Millionaire 百萬富翁	Salesman 銷售員	Persuasive 具說服力	Dinosaur 恐龍

Jokes and GIGGLES

029. Musical Claus

Why did Santa go to music school?

To improve his wrapping (rapping) skills!

LIKE REPLY

030. Reptiles' Movie

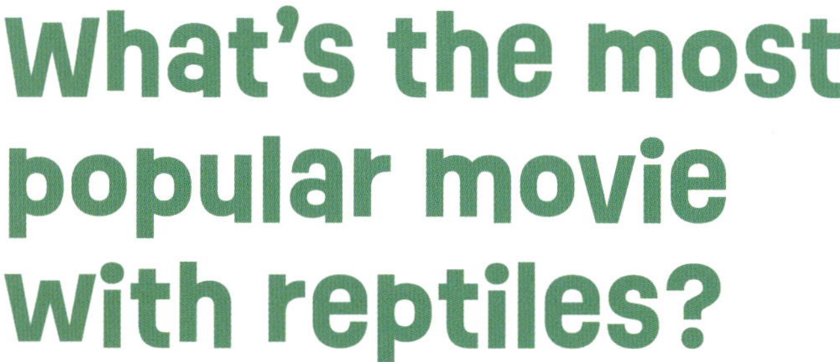

What's the most popular movie with reptiles?

The Lizard (Wizard) of Oz.

LIKE REPLY

Vocabulary Corner 實用詞彙

- Music 音樂
- Wrapping 包裝
- Reptiles 爬行動物

031. Ladder Ride

Why did the boy bring a ladder on the bus?

He wanted to go to high school.

LIKE REPLY

032. Belt Arrested

Why was the belt arrested?

Because it was holding up some pants.

LIKE REPLY

Lizard 蜥蜴	Ladder 梯	High School 高中	Arrested 被捕

033. Bad Manner

Which bird has the worst manners?

Mocking bird.

LIKE REPLY

034. Top Swimmer

What kind of horse is good at swimming?

Seahorse.

LIKE REPLY

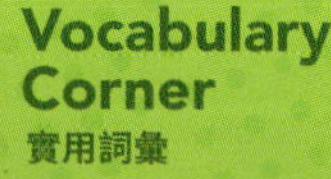

Vocabulary Corner
實用詞彙

Manner	Mocking	Good At
舉止	取笑	擅長

035. Space Currency

What currency can we use to buy coffee in space?

Starbucks.

LIKE REPLY

036. Get In Touch

What is the best way to get in touch with a fish?

Drop it a line!

LIKE REPLY

Currency 貨幣	Space 太空	Get in touch 聯絡	Drop a line 留言

037. Swift Protection

Why don't vampires attack Taylor Swift?

Because she has "Bad Blood".

LIKE REPLY

038. Perfect Gift

What is the best present?

Broken drums! You can't beat them.

LIKE REPLY

Vocabulary Corner 實用詞彙

Vampires 吸血鬼	Protection 保護	Attack 攻擊

039. Word Order

When does Friday come before Thursday?

In the dictionary.

LIKE REPLY

040. Line up

What do you call a line of men waiting to get haircuts?

A Barber-queue (Barbecue).

LIKE REPLY

Haircuts
剪頭髮

041. Bullet's Job

Why did the bullet lose its job?

It got fired.

LIKE REPLY

042. Zero Hero

How would you thank the guy who invented zero?

Thanks for nothing.

LIKE REPLY

Vocabulary Corner
實用詞彙

Bullet 子彈	Lose 失去	Invented 發明

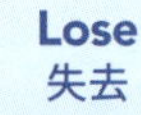

043. City Tales

What building in city has the most stories?

The public library!

LIKE REPLY

044. Magnetic Bond

What did the paper clip say to the magnet?

I find you very attractive!

LIKE REPLY

Tales 故事	Magnetic 磁性	Paper Clip 曲別針	Magnet 磁鐵

045. Battery

How much do dead batteries cost?

There should be no charge.

LIKE REPLY

046. Funny Paws

Which dog breed will always laugh at our jokes?

A Chi-ha-ha!

LIKE REPLY

Vocabulary Corner
實用詞彙

Battery 電池	Paw 爪	Dog breed 狗種

047. Silent Pages

Where do books hide when they're scared?

Under their covers.

LIKE REPLY

048. Chef's Death

Did you hear about the Italian chef who died?

He pasta-way.

LIKE REPLY

Silent 安靜

Hide 藏

Italian 意大利

Chef 廚師

049. Cat Space

Why was the cat sitting on the computer?

It wanted to keep an eye on the mouse!

LIKE REPLY

050. Hidden Secret

Why are Mexican restaurants usually kept secret?

No one will taco-bout (talk about) it.

LIKE REPLY

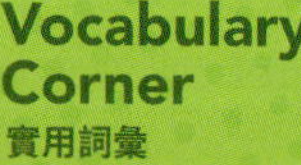

Vocabulary Corner
實用詞彙

Computer 電腦	Keep an eye 留意	Mexican 墨西哥人

051. Peaceful Skeletons

Why don't skeletons fight?

They don't have the guts.

LIKE REPLY

052. Pig Battle

What's it called when pigs compete in athletic games?

The Olympigs!

LIKE REPLY

Skeletons 骷髏	Guts 勇氣 / 內臟	Compete 競爭	Athletic 體育

FLIP AND LAUGH
but i like
053 - 072

053 - 072

053

Ocean Power

What's the strongest creature in the ocean?

- Select Your Answer! -

A Whale

B Eel

C Mussel

053 ANSWER
C
Mussel
(Muscle)

054

Cold Nuts

What kind of nuts always seem to have a cold?

- Select Your Answer! -

A Hazelnut

B Cashew

C Peanut

054 ANSWER
B
Cashew
(Achoo!)

055
Pirate's Secret

Where do pirates get their hooks?

- Select Your Answer! -

A **Book Store**

B **Drug Store**

C **Second Hand Store**

055 ANSWER
C
The second
Hand Store

056
Risky Jungle

Why shouldn't you play poker in the jungle?

- Select Your Answer! -

A
Too many bears

B
Too many snakes

C
Too many cheetahs

056 ANSWER
C
Because there were too many cheetahs!
(Cheaters)

057
Mini Tree

What kind of tree can you grow in your hand?

- Select Your Answer! -

A Maple Tree

B Palm Tree

C Pine Tree

057 ANSWER
B
Palm
Tree

058

Spy Shoes

What kind of shoes do spy wear?

- Select Your Answer! -

A Sneakers

B Running Shoes

C High Heels

058 ANSWER
A
Sneakers

059
Middle Japan

What do you find in the middle of Japan?

- Select Your Answer! -

A Red Dot

B Sushi

C Letter "P"

059 ANSWER
C
Letter "P"

060

Hungry Monster

Why did the monster eat the torch ?

- Select Your Answer! -

A

He missed breakfast.

B

He is angry!

C

He wanted a light snack.

C
He wanted a light snack.

061
Germ Nation

Which country has the most germs?

- Select Your Answer! -

Mexico

Germany

Egypt

061 ANSWER
B
Germany
(Germ, Many!)

062
Healthy Dolphins

What do dolphins eat to stay healthy??

- Select Your Answer! -

A	B	C
Fish	Seaweed	Vitamin C

C

Vitamin C

(Vitamin Sea)

063
Tree Nap

Why did the tree need to take a nap?

- Select Your Answer! -

A Classroom

B Forest

C Library

063 ANSWER
B
Forest
(For-rest)

064
Fishing Tool

What does a librarian bring when they go fishing?

- Select Your Answer! -

A
Book

B
Computer

C
Bookworm

C
Bookworm

065

Payment

How do donuts pay for their coffee?

- Select Your Answer! -

Donation

Credit Card

Cash

065 ANSWER
A
Donation
(Dough-nation)

066
Snowy Crime

What did the police say to the stealing snowman?

- Select Your Answer! -

A Freeze!

B Stop!

C Jump!

066 ANSWER
A
Freeze!

067
Bears' Shoes

Why don't bears wear shoes?

A
The shoes are too expensive!

B
They like bear feet!

C
The shoes are too big!

067 ANSWER
B
Because they prefer bear feet!
(Bare feet!)

068
Bookmark

Why does elephant use his trunk as a bookmark?

- Select Your Answer! -

It's trendy now in the jungle.

To impress others in the jungle.

His nose where to stop.

068 ANSWER
C
So he knows (hose) where he stopped reading.

069

Luxury Fish

What are the most expensive fish?

- Select Your Answer! -

A	B	C
Goldfish	Tuna Fish	Salmon Fish

069 ANSWER
A
Goldfish!

070

Ball

what kind of ball doesn't bounce back?

- Select Your Answer! -

Football

Bowling Ball

Snowball

070 ANSWER
C
Snowball

071
Breakfast Rules

What are the two things you don't eat for breakfast?

- Select Your Answer! -

A
Eggs and Toast

B
Lunch and Dinner

C
Pancakes and Sausage

071 ANSWER
B
Lunch
and Dinner

072
Birthday Gift

What doesn't a footballer want for their birthday?

- Select Your Answer! -

A	B	C
Red Card	Helmet	Hand Gloves

072 ANSWER
A
Red Card

MEMO

BUT I LIKE

GUMMY
JOKE 英文軟糖笑話 2

JOKES AND GIGGLES

073 - 112

Jokes and GIGGLES

073. Busy Readers

Why don't readers have any extra time?

They are booked.

LIKE REPLY

074. Counting

What is 3/7 chicken, 2/3 cat and 1/2 goat?

Chicago (Chi-ca-go).

Vocabulary Corner 實用詞彙

Extra 額外	Combination 組合	Chicago 芝加哥

075. Librarian's Favorite

What vegetables do librarians like?

Quiet peas (Quiet please)!

LIKE REPLY

076. Bathing Dino

Why did the dinosaur take a bath?

To become ex-stinked!

LIKE REPLY

Librarians
圖書館員

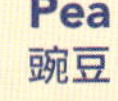
Pea
豌豆

Dinosaur
恐龍

Stinked
發臭

077. Mad Journey

How do crazy people go through the forest?

They take the psycho path.
LIKE REPLY

078. Top Geology

What do you call an awesome geologist??

A rockstar!
LIKE REPLY

079. Hot Garlic

What does garlic do when it gets hot?

Takes its cloves (clothes) off.

LIKE REPLY

080. Maths Learning

Where do New York kids learn their multiplication?

Time Square.

LIKE REPLY

Multiplication
乘法

Jokes and GIGGLES

081. Sleepy Meal

What part of a meal makes you the most sleepy?

Napkin (Nap-kin).

LIKE REPLY

082. Chimney's Talk

What did the old chimney say to the young chimney?

You're too little to smoke.

LIKE REPLY

Vocabulary Corner
實用詞彙

Sleepy	Meal	Napkin
昏昏欲睡	餐	餐巾

083. Special Truck

What do you call a truck made out of wood ?

It wooden (wouldn't) work.
LIKE REPLY

084. No Tree Invites

Why do you never want to invite a tree to your party?

Because they never leave (leaf) when you want them to.
LIKE REPLY

Chimney 煙囪
Truck 貨車
Wood 木頭
Invite 邀請

085. Musical Computer

What do you call a singing laptop?

A Dell (Adele).

LIKE REPLY

086. Magic Tricks

What did the fisherman say to the magician?

Pick a cod (card), pick a cod (card).

LIKE REPLY

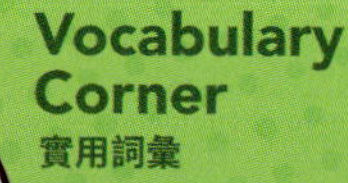

Vocabulary Corner
實用詞彙

Laptop 手提電腦	Fisherman 漁夫	Magician 魔術師

087. Solves Equations

What do you call a cat solving two math problems?

A meow-ti-tasker (multitasker) !

LIKE REPLY

088. April's Exhaustion

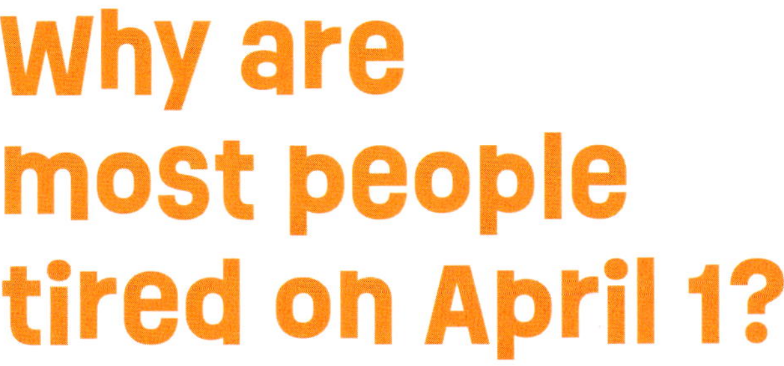

Why are most people tired on April 1?

They've just finished a 31-day March.

LIKE REPLY

Cod	Equations	Multitasker	Exhaustion
鱈魚	方程式	多任務處理者	疲勞

089. Bird's Greeting

How do birds say hello?

Goose Bump.

LIKE REPLY

090. Seagulls' Home

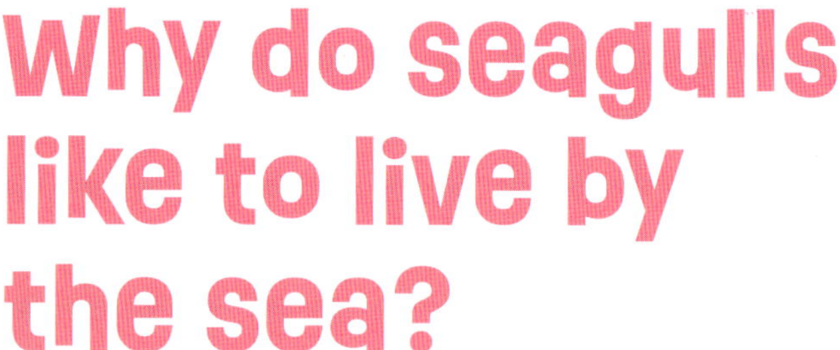

Why do seagulls like to live by the sea?

Because if they lived by the bay, they would be bagels!

Vocabulary Corner
實用詞彙

Greeting	Goose Bump	Seagull
問候	雞皮疙瘩	海鷗

091. Computer Diet

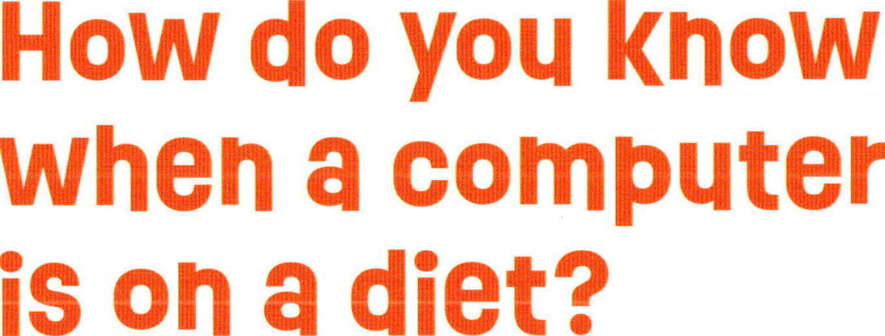

How do you know when a computer is on a diet?

It quits eating after only one byte (bite).

LIKE REPLY

092. Cow Without Legs

What do you call a cow with no legs?

The ground beef.

LIKE REPLY

Bay 海灣	Bagel 貝果	Diet 節食	Ground Beef 碎牛肉

093. Best McDonald's Day

What is the best day to visit McDonalds?

Friday (Fry-Day).

LIKE REPLY

094. Kangaroo Birthday

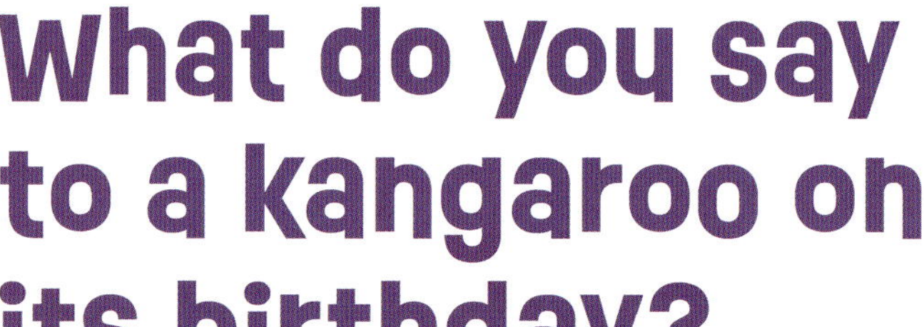

What do you say to a kangaroo on its birthday?

Hoppy (Happy) birthday!

LIKE REPLY

Vocabulary Corner
實用詞彙

Visit	Kangaroo	Birthday
訪問	袋鼠	生日

095. A+ for Steak

What do you say to steak that have good school report?

Well done.

LIKE REPLY

096. Eggs in Autumn

Why does Humpty Dumpty love autumn so much?

Because he had a great fall.

LIKE REPLY

Humpty Dumpty
矮胖子

Jokes and GIGGLES

097. Lost Cow

What did the farmer say when he lost a cow?

What a miss-steak (mistake).

LIKE REPLY

098. Shutdown

Why did the gym close down?

It just didn't work out.

LIKE REPLY

Vocabulary Corner
實用詞彙

Lost 丟失	Mistake 錯誤	Shutdown 關閉

099. French Dining

Why do French people eat snails?

They don't like fast food.

LIKE REPLY

100. Sheep's Ambition

What is a sheep's ultimate goal?

To wool (rule) the world!

LIKE REPLY

Work Out 健身 / 事情發展	French 法國	Ambition 抱負	Ultimate 終極

101. Battle Squid

How does a squid go into battle?

Well armed.

LIKE REPLY

102. Bad Luck Map

Why did the map always lose at poker?

It always folded.

LIKE REPLY

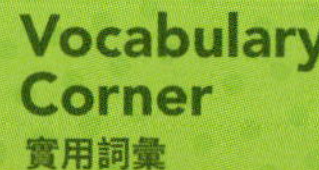

Vocabulary Corner
實用詞彙

Squid 魷魚	Battle 戰鬥	Poker 德州撲克

103. Chill Vibes

Why do slothes always make great friends?

Because they like to hang out.

LIKE REPLY

104. Winter Migration

Why do birds fly south in the winter?

It's faster than walking.

LIKE REPLY

Folded 棄牌 / 折疊	Chill Vibe 放鬆氛圍	Slothes 樹懶	Migration 遷徙

105. Three Eyes Alien

What do you call an alien with three eyes?

Aliiien.

LIKE REPLY

106. Dentist Visit

Why did the Oreo go to the dentist?

Because he lost his filling.

Vocabulary Corner
實用詞彙

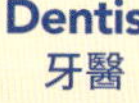

Alien	Dentist	Filling
外星人	牙醫	補牙 / 餡

107. Festive Conversation

What did one Xmas bauble say to the other?

I like hanging with you

LIKE REPLY

108. Silent Skeletons

Why are skeletons so calm?

Because nothing gets under their skin.

LIKE REPLY

Festive 節日	Conversation 交談	Xmas Bauble 聖誕裝飾球	Calm 冷靜

109. Sick Bird

What do you give a sick bird?

Tweetment (Treament).

LIKE REPLY

110. Parallel Problems

Why was the parallel line always in trouble?

Because it could never stay straight.

LIKE REPLY

Vocabulary Corner
實用詞彙

Tweet 會計師	Treatment 治療	Parallel 平行

111. Cereal Promotion

Why did the cereal get promoted at work?

Because it was oat-standing (outstanding)!
LIKE REPLY

112. Phone Proposal

How did the mobile phone propose to his girlfriend?

He gave her a ring.
LIKE REPLY

Stay Straight 保持直線 / 誠實

Cereal 穀物

Oat 燕麥

Propose 求婚

FLIP AND LAUGH
but i like
113 - 132

FLIP AND LAUGH

but i like

113 - 132

113

Monster Feast

On which day do monster eat people?

- Select Your Answer! -

Tuesday

Thursday

Sunday

113 ANSWER
A
Tuesday
(Chewsday)

114
Daily Shaves

Who can shave ten times a day and still have a beard?

- Select Your Answer! -

A Ben

B Bob

C Barber

114 ANSWER
C
Barber

115
Icy Answer

How do you spell 'hard water' using only three letters?

- Select Your Answer! -

A D,S,E

B M,E,W

C I,E,C

115 ANSWER
C
I,E,C
(I-C-E)

113
Shopping Day

Where does Superman love to shop?

- Select Your Answer! -

A
Beauty Salon

B
Fast Food Shop

C
Supermarket

116 ANSWER
C
Supermarket

117
Bank's Day

Why did the man bring his watch to the bank?

- Select Your Answer! -

A. To pay bills.

B. To save time.

C. To invest.

B
To save time.

117
Hamburgers Party

Where do hamburgers dance?

- Select Your Answer! -

A
Fridge!

B
Kitchen!

C
Meatball!

C
Meat-ball!

119

Perfect Fit

Which table fits in the fridge?

- Select Your Answer! -

A	B	C
Bar Table	Vegetable	Round Table

119 ANSWER
B
Vegetable
(Veg-table)

120
Egypt Baby

Why was the baby in Egypt?

- Select Your Answer! -

A Looking for its mummy.

B The care centre was full.

C The baby wanted to travel.

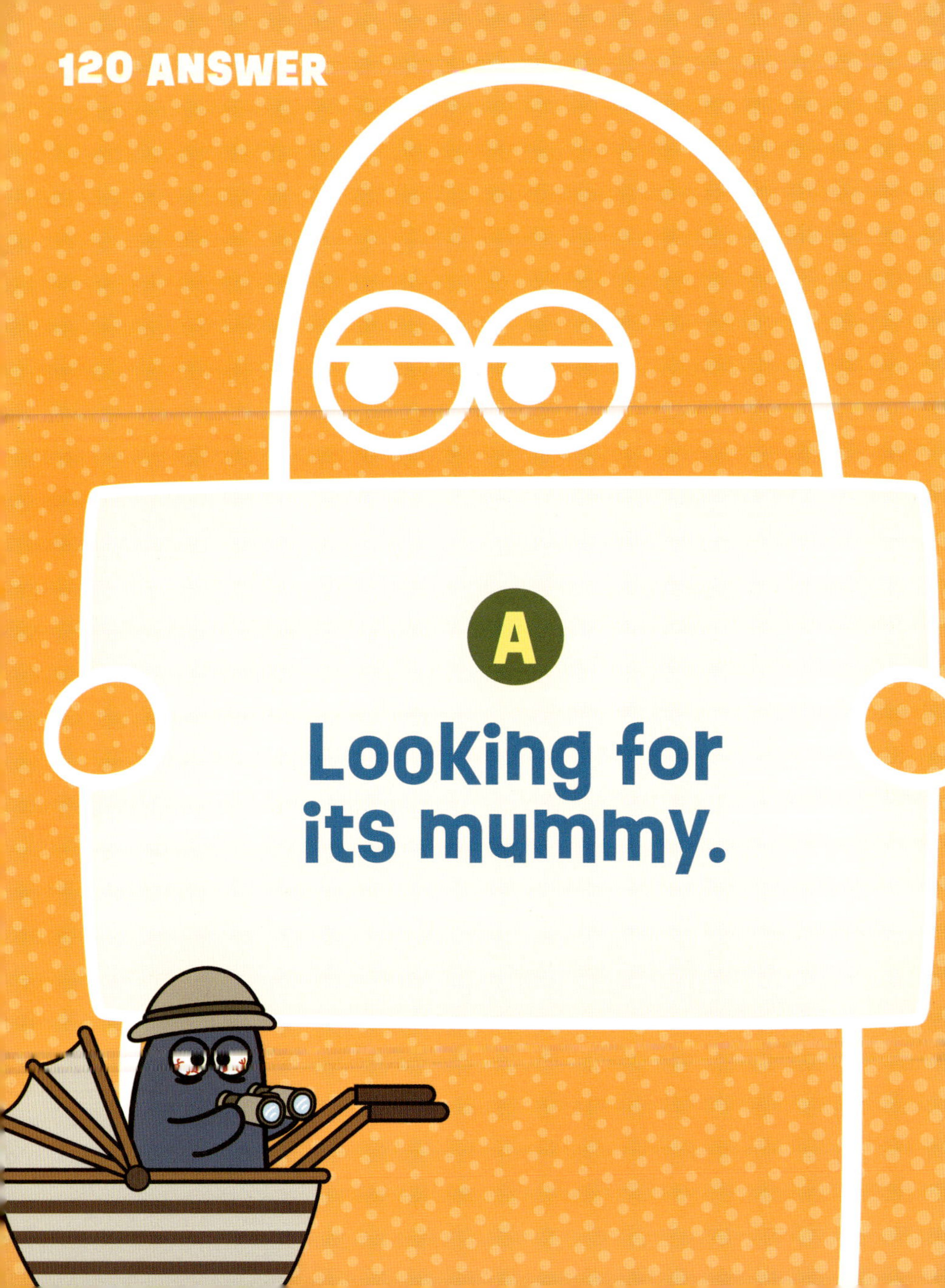
120 ANSWER
A
Looking for its mummy.

121

Talking Boards

How do billboards talk?

- Select Your Answer! -

A
By whistle

B
By Japanese

C
Sign Lanuage

121 ANSWER
C
Sign
Lanuage

122
Lighter

What lights up a stadium??

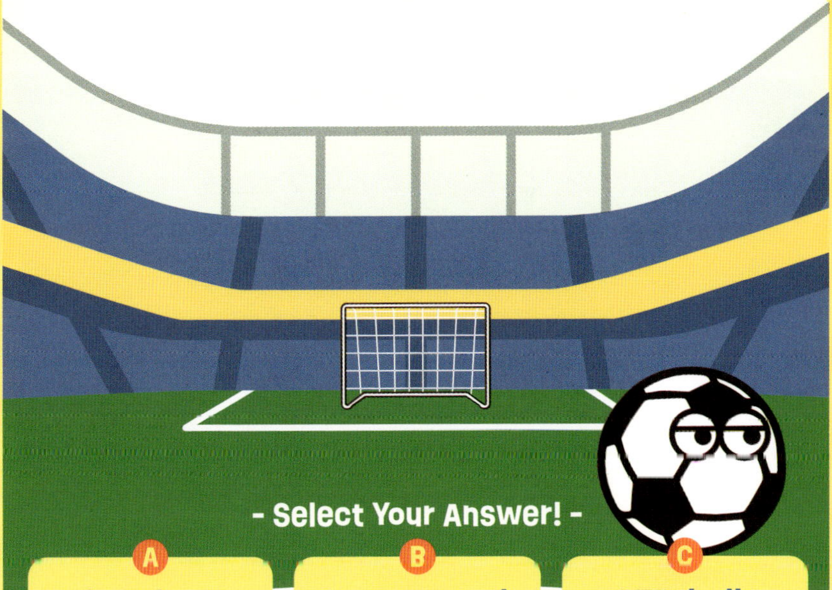

- Select Your Answer! -

A. Floor lamps

B. Soccer match

C. LED bulb

B
Soccer
Match

123
Paper's Humor

What do you call a joke about paper?

- Select Your Answer! -

A It's amazing!

B It's terrible!

C It's annoying!

B
It's terrible!
(Tearable!)
Joke
Joke

124
Sweet Keys

What kind of keys are sweet?

- Select Your Answer! -

A Turkey

B Cookie

C Monkey

124 ANSWER
B
Cookie
(Coo-key)

125
Smile!

How do you get a mouse to smile?

- Select Your Answer! -

A

126
Negativity

What's the most negative month in the fall?

- Select Your Answer! -

A	B	C
September	October	November

C
NO-vember

127
Art Tea

Why do artists drink tea?

- Select Your Answer! -

Creativity.

It makes them healthy.

It makes them silly.

127 ANSWER
A
Creativity
(Creativi-tea)

128
Grape Accident

What did the grape do when it got stepped on?

- Select Your Answer! -

A It makes the grapes injured.

B It lets out a little wine.

C It makes the grapes scream.

B
It lets out a little wine.
(whine)

129

Chickens Study

What do chickens study in school?

- Select Your Answer! -

A 

Science

B 

Economic

C 

History

129 ANSWER
B
Ecohomic
(Egg-onomic)

130
Fairy tale Veggie

What do you call a mythical veggie?

- Select Your Answer! -

A
Pumpkin

B
Onion

C
Unicorn

130 ANSWER
C
Unicorn
(Uni-corn)

131

Baby Tree

Where do baby tree go to learn?

- Select Your Answer! -

A Elementary School

B Pastry School

C Swimming School

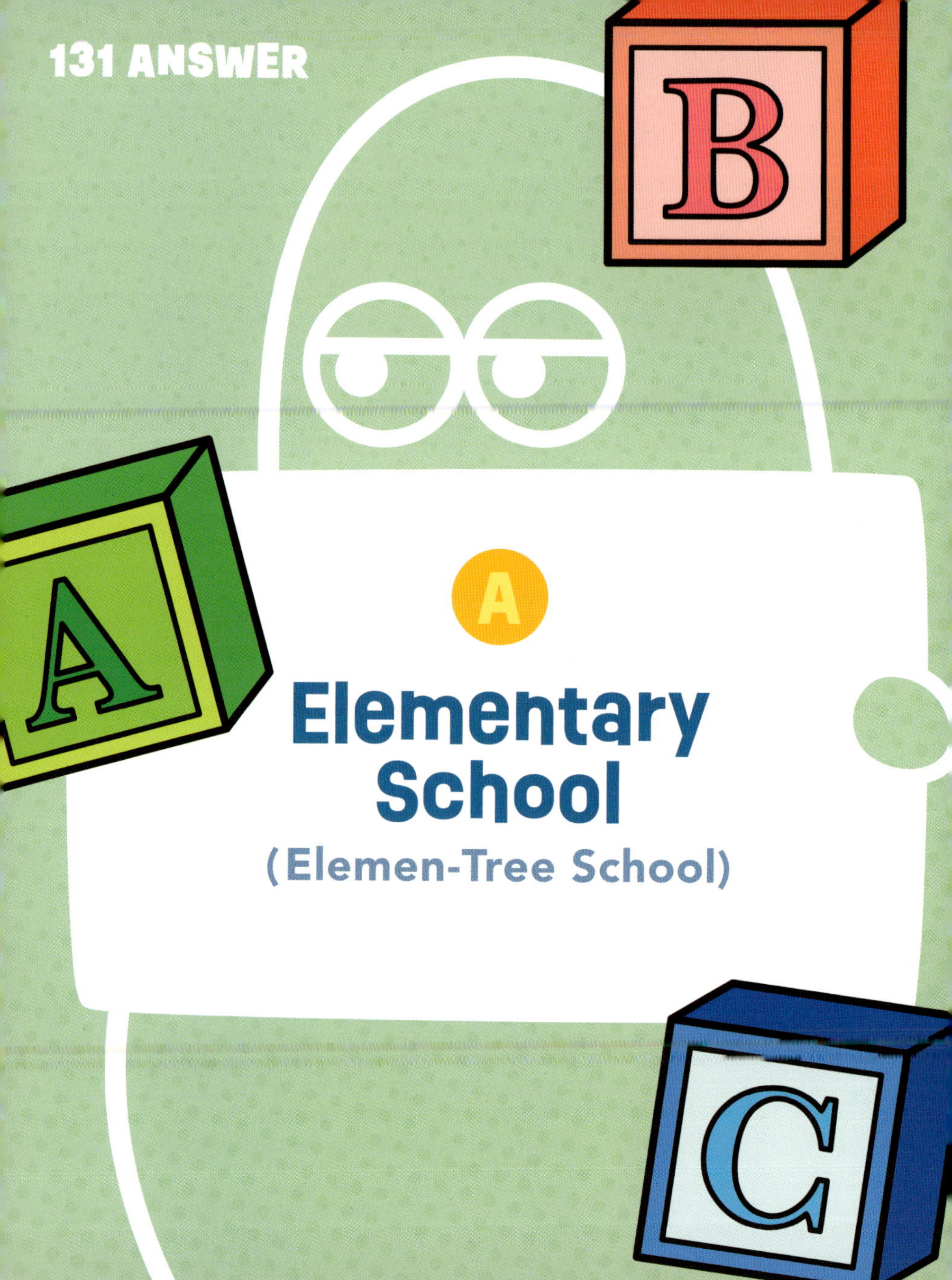

A

Elementary School

(Elemen-Tree School)

132
Sticky Job

What kind of job is easy to stick to?

- Select Your Answer! -

A
Glue Factory Worker

Pizza Chef

Dog Trainer

132 ANSWER
A
Glue Factory
Worker!

MEMO

BUT I LIKE

GUMMY
Joke 英文軟糖笑話 2

JOKES AND GIGGLES

133 - 172

133. Pumpkin's Game

What is a pumpkin's favorite sport?

Squash!

LIKE REPLY

134. Legal Name

What did the lawyer name her daughter?

Sue!

LIKE REPLY

Vocabulary Corner
實用詞彙

Squash	Lawyer	Sue
壁球 / 南瓜	律師	控告 / 女生名字

135. Tiger Meal

Why don't tiger like fast food?

Because they can't catch it.

LIKE REPLY

136. Population Boom

Which country have a rapid-growing population?

Ireland because every day it's Dublin (doubling).

LIKE REPLY

Fast Food 快餐	Population 人口	Rapid 快速	Dublin 都柏林

137. Spice Freeze

Why do peppers hate winter?

They get a little chili (chilly).

LIKE REPLY

138. Kitchen Kungfu

Why is it hard to learn chinese cooking?

They get so much home-wok (homework).

LIKE REPLY

Vocabulary Corner
實用詞彙

Pepper	Chilly	Wok
甜椒	辣椒 / 冷	鍋

139. Wizard Fall

What do you call a wizard who fell down the stairs?

Tumble-dore (Dumbledore from "Harry Potter").

LIKE REPLY

140. Fungi Bloom

What's the best way for fungi to grow?

You must give it as mushroom (much room) as possible!

LIKE REPLY

Wizard 魔法師	Stairs 樓梯	Fungi 真菌類植物	Grow 生長

141. Fish Serve

Why don't fish play tennis?

They're scared of the net!

LIKE REPLY

142. Dog's Bath

What does a dog use to wash his fur?

Shampoo-dle (poodle).

LIKE REPLY

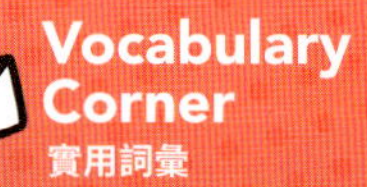

Vocabulary Corner
實用詞彙

Serve 發球	Net 網	Poodle 貴賓狗

143. Wet Alphabet

Which letter of the alphabet has the most water?

The "C" (Sea).

LIKE REPLY

144. Color Clue

When do you go at red and stop at green?

When you're eating a watermelon!

LIKE REPLY

Fur 煙囪	Alphabet 字母	Clue 線索	Stop 停止

145. Chinese Rap

If Korean pop is K-Pop, what is Chinese rap?

C-Rap (Crap).

LIKE REPLY

146. Tree's Bank

What did the tree do when the bank closed?

It started its own branch.

LIKE REPLY

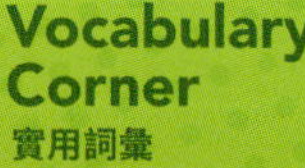

Vocabulary Corner
實用詞彙

Korean 韓國人	Bank 銀行	Branch 分行

147. Frosty Robbery

What makes a cold such a bad robber?

They're too easy to catch.

LIKE REPLY

148. Broke Greens

Why was the vegetable broke?

It had no celery (salary).

LIKE REPLY

Frosty 結霜	Robber 搶匪	Broke 破產	Celery 芹菜

149. Beauty Contest

Who won the skeleton beauty contest?

No bodies.

LIKE REPLY

150. Endless Feast

In which country can you never stop eating?

Hungary.

LIKE REPLY

Vocabulary Corner
實用詞彙

Skeleton	Contest	Endless
骷髏骨	比賽	無盡

151. Cow Chat

What do cows use in WhatsApp messages?

Emoo-ojis (emoji)!

LIKE REPLY

152. Cool Player

Who is the coolest player in Premier League?

Cold Palmer (Cole Palmer).

LIKE REPLY

Feast 盛宴	Chat 聊天	Wtsapp 訊應用程式	League 聯賽

153. Tea Relocation

Why did the tea couple move to town?

They thought it was a lovely communi-tea (community).

LIKE REPLY

154. Fake Apple

What kind of apple isn't an apple?

A pineapple

LIKE REPLY

Vocabulary Corner
實用詞彙

Relocation 搬遷	Couple 情侶	Town 城市

155. Yummy Road

Why did the girl smear peanut butter on the road?

To go with the traffic jam!
LIKE REPLY

156. Dark Vision

Why doesn't Voldemort wear glasses?

Nobody nose!
LIKE REPLY

Fake 假的

Smear 塗抹

Peanut Butter 花生醬

Vision 視力

157. Tidy Room

Why C.Ronaldo's bedroom always tidy?

Because he's not Messi.

LIKE REPLY

158. Favorite App

What's Thanos' favourite app on his phone?

Snapchat!

LIKE REPLY

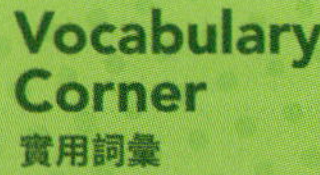

Vocabulary Corner
實用詞彙

Tidy	Ronaldo	Thanos
整齊	葡萄牙球員	漫威反派

159. Ocean Startup

How do fish go into business?

They start on a small scale.

LIKE REPLY

160. Jurassic Cut

How does a T-rex cut wood?

With a dino-saw!

LIKE REPLY

Startup 創業	Scale 規模 / 魚鱗	Jurassic 侏羅紀	Saw 鋸

161. Log Wheels

Did you hear about the car with logs for wheels?

It wooden (wouldn't) go.

LIKE REPLY

162. Cat Comedy

What does the cat say after making a joke?

Just kitten (kidding)!

LIKE REPLY

Vocabulary Corner
實用詞彙

Log 木材	Wheel 車輪	Comedy 喜劇

163. Spooky Lies

Why are ghosts bad liars?

They're totally see through.

LIKE REPLY

164. Pork Thief

What do you call a pig who steals stuff?

A ham-burglar!

LIKE REPLY

Spooky 驚悚	Liar 說謊者	Steal 偷竊	Burglar 小偷

165. Space Breakup

What does an astronaut call his ex from space?

SpaceX (Ex).

LIKE REPLY

166. Choco Education

Why did the M&M go to school?

Because he really wanted to be a "Smartie"!

LIKE REPLY

Vocabulary Corner
實用詞彙

Breakup	Astronaut	Space
分手	太空人	太空

167. Spring Season

Why do trees love spring?

It makes them feel re-leaved (relief).

LIKE REPLY

168. Slow Celebration

What do turtles do on their birthdays?

They shell-ebrate (celebrate).

LIKE REPLY

Education 教育	Spring 春天	Relief 舒解	Turtle 烏龜

169. Lemon Blues

What do you call a sad lemon?

A le-moan (lemon).

LIKE REPLY

170. Party Scoop

Why does everyone invite ice cream to the party?

Because it's so cool.

LIKE REPLY

Vocabulary Corner
實用詞彙

Lemon 檸檬

Moan 發牢騷

Scoop 一勺

171. Nurse Art

Want to know why nurses like red crayons?

Sometimes they have to draw blood.

LIKE REPLY

172. Favorite Soda

What's a frog's favourite soda?

Croak-a-Cola!

LIKE REPLY

Nurse 護士	Crayon 蠟筆	Draw Blood 抽血	Soa 視力

BUT i LIKE

網店專區

ideapublication.com

01 精選人氣書籍

《無聊爛 GAG 怪3》

點解搞笑嘅嘢要講三次？

因為笑到 Gag Gag Gag ！

《無聊爛 GAG 怪2》

來吧！雙倍搞笑，

加強版笑彈放送！

《無聊爛 GAG 怪》

睇到反晒白眼！

全中文笑話大集合！

02 ButiLike 眼啤熊 Figure

12cm × 8cm × 7cm

初回限定版

黑色幽默版

＊圖片只供參考，一切以實物為準

03 **ButiLike**
四色帆布袋
40.5cm × 38.5cm（高 × 闊）

04 **ButiLike 防水膠貼系列**
約 7.5cm × 8.5cm 範圍內

第一彈
動物系列

第二彈
食物系列

第三彈
精靈系列

05 **ButiLike「幽」襪系列**

06 **ButiLike 透明書夾**

全店凡購滿$400全港免運費！
BUTiLIKE 網店專區

GUMMY Joke 英文軟糖笑話 2

免責聲明：
本書所有內容，均為作者個人意見，並不完全代表本出版社立場。

DESIGNED IN HONG KONG. PRINTED IN CHINA. IDEAPUBLICATION.COM BY IDEA PUBLICATION 2025.

AUTHOR	But I Like (_butilike)
EDITOR	點子出版編輯部
PROOFREADER	YC Fish
DESIGNER	陳希頤 Tiffany Chan
PRODUCTION	點子出版 Idea Publication www.ideapublication.com
PUBLISHER	點子出版 Idea Publication
ADDRESS	荃灣海盛路 11 號 One MidTown 13 樓 20 室
INQUIRY	info@idea-publication.com
PRINTER	CP Printing Limited
ADDRESS	北角健康東街 39 號柯達大廈二座 17 樓 8 室
INQUIRY	2154 4242
DISTRIBUTOR	泛華發行代理有限公司
ADDRESS	將軍澳工業邨駿昌街 7 號 2 樓
INQUIRY	gccd@singtaonewscorp.com
PUBLICATION DATE	2025 年 11 月 30 日 (第二版)
ISBN	978-988-70671-5-3
FIXED PRICE	$98

點子出版
IDEA PUBLICATION

BÜT
i LIKE

GUMMY

JOKE 英文軟糖笑話 2